TOUGH TRUCKS
The Crane

Written by Frances Ann Ladd
Illustrated by Bill Alger and Keiron Ward

SCHOLASTIC INC.
New York   Toronto   London   Auckland   Sydney
Mexico City   New Delhi   Hong Kong   Buenos Aires

ISBN 0-439-48732-3

Published by Scholastic Inc.
SCHOLASTIC and associated logos are trademarks and/or registered trademarks of Scholastic Inc.

10 9 8 7 6 5 4 3 2 1   03 04 05 06 07 08

Cover design by Maria Stasavage
Interior design by Bethany Dixon

Printed in the U.S.A.
First printing, August 2003

Dear Family Members:

Welcome to the TONKA Tough Trucks series! Your child will have the opportunity to learn more about how things work while improving reading skills. I know that kids like trucks because they are big and interesting. They also like big and interesting words like the ones in this book. TONKA truck books provide an introduction to nonfiction text—the kind of writing your child will meet in textbooks and even on the Internet. Here are suggestions for helping your child *before, during,* and *after* reading.

Before
- Look at the cover and pictures and have your child predict what the story is about.
- Be word watchers. Look for new and challenging vocabulary words and talk about what the words mean.

During
- Encourage your child to use phonics skills to sound out new words.
- Provide the word for your child, especially when it is a technical one, when more assistance is needed so that he or she does not struggle and the experience of reading with you is a positive one.

After
- Have your child keep lists of interesting and favorite words—there are so many choices in this book.
- Encourage your child to read the book over and over again. Brothers, sisters, grandparents, and even teddy bears make a great audience. Repeated readings develop confidence in young readers.
- Talk about the stories. Ask and answer questions.
- Visit a construction site and practice using new vocabulary words.

I do hope that you and your child enjoy the big trucks, big words, and big ideas in this book!

—Francie Alexander
Chief Academic Officer
Scholastic Education

A crane is the tallest
thing on a construction site!

Cranes lift and move heavy loads.
Some cranes can lift loads heavier than 500 tons.
That is like lifting 100 elephants at once!

Some cranes are so tall that workers like to put a Christmas tree or a flag on top of them!

The operator sits in the cab. And sits and sits. He has a lot of work to do!

It might make you think of a giraffe eating her lunch at the zoo!

Have you ever raised a flag on a flagpole? If you have, you used a small pulley.

A pulley is a wheel with a grooved rim.
A chain or rope runs over the wheel. Pulleys make lifting easier.

There are all kinds of cranes, with different names.
They are named for the tool on the crane's pulley.

A crane can have a wrecking ball on it. Workers call this kind of crane a Wrecking Ball.

Hooks are cranes with a big hook on them!

Some cranes are called Clamshells. Watch out! That huge Clamshell looks hungry!

Next stop is the service station!